Catherine Stacey

The Picnic

Nightingale Books

A CIP catalogue record for this title is
available from the British Library.
ISBN 978-1-83875-268-2

Nightingale Books is an imprint of
Pegasus Elliot MacKenzie Publishers Ltd.
www.pegasuspublishers.com

First Published in 2023

Nightingale Books
Sheraton House Castle Park
Cambridge England

Printed & Bound in Great Britain

For my son Marlen, who's wonderful imagination inspires me every day.

There once was a squirrel who lived in a tree.

He was as happy as any squirrel could possibly be.

He lived in a big old oak tree, with loads of leaves which kept him dry when it rained, and gave him shade on hot sunny days. There were many branches for him to swing from, climb on and jump off of, with a lovely hole in the trunk of the tree which made for a super cosy home. Best of all, there were endless amounts of acorns which he could nibble on all day long (and store over the winter) so he never went hungry.

Squirrel was so very happy in his perfect tree, but he sometimes felt like something was missing. He longed to try something new! As much as he adored his beloved nuts, he was keen to try something different. But what?? Perhaps a picnic with his dearest friends would help him find a fabulous new treat?!

With perfect timing, his neighbour, Bird, flitted into her nearby tree and began chomping on something.

"What are you eating there, dear Bird?" Squirrel asked.

Do you know what Bird was eating? Can you guess?

"Just my morning worms", Bird replied.

"Eeeeeeuuuuugh!" thought Squirrel, not sure if worms were for him — they were too slimy, sludgy, sandy, squiggly and wriggly... but, remembering that he needed to try something new, he decided to keep an open mind.

"Would you like to join me for a picnic?," asked Squirrel.

"Why that would be wonderful," tweeted Bird, and grabbing her worms in her beautiful beak, she flew onto squirrels branch.

At that very moment they heard a rustling in the leaves on the ground below. Who could it be?

It was their dear friend Hedgehog!

"Hello down there our prickly little buddy!," cried Squirrel.
"Whatever are you doing?"

"Just grabbing my yummy breakfast," replied Hedgehog.

"Well fancy that! We were just saying that we are going to have
a picnic. Would you like to join us?" said Squirrel

"Yes, certainly!" replied Hedgehog. "I'm having a very good
forage this morning and there is plenty of food for all of us!"

As quick as a flash, Squirrel sped down the tree to see what delights awaited him. Bird excitedly followed closely behind him.

What was Hedgehog eating? Can you guess?

Squirrel was expecting something glorious and scrumptious, but all he could see were lots of creepy crawly beetles! "Was the delicious food underneath them perhaps?", wondered Squirrel.

"Nothing could possibly be better than a mouthful of beetles!" said Hedgehog, who was very happy with his haul.

A mouthful of beetles???? Squirrel begged to differ! Beetles were gooey, creepy, crawly and crunchy!

Poor Squirrel was looking a bit green around his fuzzy face at the thought of munching down on them, but he reminded himself that he needed to try something new, and the three friends sat down to begin their picnic.

Squirrel tentatively picked up a wriggly worm, closed his eyes, and was just about to pop it in his mouth when they heard the leaves on a big bush move right in front of them!!

Who or what, was coming out of it?!

Was it an **enormous snappy** crocodile?

A **big, roaring stomping** dinosaur?

A **giant hairy** spider?!?

The friends held onto each other tightly... waiting!

And out popped...

The cutest little teddy bear!!! He had big shiny brown eyes, was wearing the sweetest little waistcoat, and in his arms were a fluffy blanket and a huge wicker basket.

But the poor bear looked very sad indeed.

"Oh dear Bear, why are you crying?" asked Squirrel

"I am lost!", cried the bear in between floods of tears. "You see, every year we hold our teddy bear's picnic, and I was up all night baking and making all sorts of scrummy treats for the party, but I lost my way this morning and now I can't find the rest of the teddy bears! I have no-one to picnic with." Sobbed Bear.

The friends gathered round the teddy bear and gave him a big hug.

"Well, as it happens Mr. Bear, we are just about to have a little picnic ourselves, and we would love it if you joined us. We only have acorns, worms and beetles but you are welcome to any of them," said Squirrel excitedly.

The bear's face broke into the biggest, fuzziest smile and he clapped his hands with joy! "I would love to!" he cried.

And with a flick of his teddy wrists he shook the blanket out and let it gently float to the ground – it was the most perfect picnic blanket! They all sat down and Bear opened up his basket and laid out the most delicious treats the friends had ever seen!

There were crunchy apples, squishy oranges, scones with cream and jam, pecan nut cookies, cheese sandwiches, blueberry muffins and the most enormous chocolate cake!

"What a feast," thought the friends excitedly!

My Big Sandcastle

by Anne Giulieri
illustrated by Susy Boyer

"Look, Mum!" said Alex.
"The sand can go here."

"Look, Mum!" said Alex.
"The tunnel can go here."

"Look, Mum!" said Alex.
"The rocks can go here."

"Look, Mum!" said Alex.
"The sticks can go here."

"Look, Mum!" said Alex.
"The leaves can go here."

"Look, Mum!" said Alex.
"The water can go here."

12

13

"Look, Mum!" said Alex.
"The wood can go here."

15

"Look!" said Alex.

"Here is my big sandcastle."